THE SNAKE'S TALES

BY MARGUERITE W. DAVOL

ILLUSTRATED BY YUMI HEO

ORCHARD BOOKS • NEW YORK • AN IMPRINT OF SCHOLASTIC INC.

IN MEMORY OF STEPHEN

AND HIS STORIES (1928 – 1982)

—M.W.D.

MISS MARGE, A DEDICATION

FOR A JAR OF YOUR RASPBERRY JAM

—Y.H.

THE SNAKE'S TALES IS AN ORIGINAL TALE SUGGESTED BY "THE STORYTELLING STONE," A TRADITIONAL SENECA TALE.

Text copyright © 2002 by Marguerite W. Davol
Illustrations copyright © 2002 by Yumi Heo

LIBRARY OF CONGRESS CATALOGING-IN-PUBLICATION DATA
Davol, Marguerite W.
The snake's tales / by Marguerite W. Davol ; illustrated by Yumi Heo. – 1st ed.   p.   cm.
Summary: In the time before stories, two children meet a snake who offers to trade tales for their fruit.
ISBN 0-439-31769-X
[1. Snakes—Fiction. 2. Storytelling—Fiction.] I. Heo, Yumi, ill. II. Title.   PZ7.D32155 Sn 2002
[Fic]—dc21   2001133072

10 9 8 7 6 5 4 3 2 1   02 03 04 05 06

Printed in Singapore   46
First edition, September 2002

Book design by Marijka Kostiw
The text of this book is set in Clois Old Style.
The illustrations are pencil and oil.

WAY BACK IN TIME THERE WERE *NO* STORIES.

SEASON AFTER SEASON, THE EARTH TURNED FROM DAY TO NIGHT TO DAY. PEOPLE WORKED AND ATE, SLEPT AND WOKE. BUT THEY DIDN'T TELL STORIES. BELIEVE IT OR NOT, PEOPLE SIMPLY DIDN'T KNOW WHAT STORIES WERE! SO HOW DID STORIES FINALLY BEGIN? LISTEN, AND I'LL TELL YOU.

NCE UPON THE TIME OF *NO* STORIES, a family lived at the edge of a forest. Each day Papa gathered his goats and herded them to a distant meadow. "Hi-yi," he would call. "Here's grass, green and sweet. Eat and grow fat." Papa passed the long hours staring at the distant hills, the sky. Sometimes he played his fipple flute. But never a story crossed his mind.

Each day Mama cooked and cared for their children, Beno and Allita. She spent long hours spinning wool, then weaving the yarn she'd dyed into tapestries with intricate pictures and patterns. But never a story entered her mind.

One summer morning, Mama called her son. "Strawberries are ripe in the field on the far side of the forest," she said. "Pick enough berries to fill this basket, Beno, and we'll have strawberry preserves to spread on our bread tonight."

So Beno took the basket and tramped through the forest. When he found the strawberry patch, Beno began to pick the juicy red fruits, pausing every now and then to pop a berry into his mouth. Mm-mmm, were they good! He picked until his basket was full.

Heading home, Beno came upon a clearing in the forest that he'd never seen before. In the middle was a large, flat stone, just the right size to sit upon and rest. Beno sat down. But he didn't notice the snake coiled around the base of the stone until it glided up beside him.

"Hello, young fellow," the snake said.

"Hello, snake," Beno replied.

Leaning over the basket, the snake hissed, "Those s-s-strawberries-s-s look s-s-sweet!"

"They are," said Beno.

The snake looked at Beno, its eyes gleaming. "Give me your s-s-strawberries and I'll tell you s-s-stories," it said.

"Stories?" Beno had never heard of stories. What were they? He was very curious, but he hesitated. The strawberries were for supper that night.

Beno stared at the snake, wondering. Finally he said, "Oh . . . all right. Take some strawberries and tell me what stories are."

And so the snake began to weave its tales. It told stories about how the stars once were bees and what makes a rose smell sweet. It told stories about why monkeys live in trees and what lizards like to eat. After each tale — shloop, shlup — the snake ate strawberries.

Captivated, Beno listened for hours. Then he looked down at his basket. "Oh, no!" he gasped. "The strawberries are all eaten!" He looked up and saw that the sun hung low in the west. "It's late. I must hurry home or Mama will be worried." Grabbing his empty basket, Beno dashed off through the forest.

The snake flipped its tail — swish, swash — then slithered away.

When Mama saw the empty basket, she exclaimed, "No strawberries?"

Beno didn't want to tell a lie, so he said, "The snake ate them."

"A snake?" Mama asked doubtfully. She didn't believe him. And Beno was sure Mama never would believe him if he told her about stories. He said nothing more, but kept thinking about the snake's tales, puzzling over each of them.

When Papa came home that night, the family ate their supper of bread and cheese. With no strawberry preserves.

One midsummer day, Mama called her daughter. "Raspberries are ripe in the bushes on the other side of the forest," she said. "Pick enough to fill this basket, Allita, and we'll have raspberries and cream for supper tonight."

Allita took the basket and skipped through the forest. Upon reaching the berry bushes, she began to pick the plump red raspberries. She picked and picked, popping a berry into her mouth every so often. Mm-mmm, so fragrant and sweet! When her basket was full, she headed for home.

Allita happened upon a clearing in the forest, a clearing she had never seen before. She saw a large, flat stone that looked just right to rest upon. She sat down. But Allita didn't notice the snake coiled around the base of the stone until it glided up beside her.

"Good day, young miss."

"Good day to you, snake," she said.

Leaning over her basket, the snake hissed, "Those ras-s-spberries-s-s look s-s-sweet!"

"They are," said Allita.

Its eyes glittering, the snake said, "Give me your ras-s-spberries-s-s and I'll tell you s-s-stories."

Like Beno, Allita had never heard of stories. She was very curious, but she hesitated. Finally, though, Allita nodded. "Take some of the raspberries," she said, "and tell me what stories are."

And so the snake began to weave its tales. It told stories about where fireflies go by day and what makes the sky blue. It told stories about why frogs croak and owls ask "Whoo, whoo?" In between stories — shloop, shlup — the snake ate raspberries.

Mesmerized, Allita listened for hours. As the sun slid behind the trees, she saw that her basket was empty. "Oh, no! All the berries are gone. And it's getting late. I must hurry, or Mama will be worried." She picked up the basket and ran toward home.

The snake flipped its tail — swish, swash — and slithered away.

When Allita returned, Mama looked at the empty basket. "No raspberries?" she exclaimed.

Allita, who never told a lie, said, "Oh, Mama, the snake ate them."

"The snake ate them?" Mama repeated, shaking her head. And Allita knew Mama would never believe her, so she said nothing about the snake's stories. Instead, she kept all of them to herself, trying hard to remember each one.

That night the family ate cheese and bread for supper. With no raspberries and cream.

One day early in the fall, Mama looked from Allita to Beno and back again. This time she would send *both* of them. "Apples are ripe in the orchard on the other side of the forest," she said. "Fill this large basket, children, and tonight we'll have apple pie for dessert."

So Allita and Beno strolled through the forest until they found the apple orchard. Stretching tall, they pulled the round, red fruit from the trees. They picked and picked until the basket was full. And heavy. Each of them hoisted one side of the basket, and as they walked, each ate a juicy apple.

Now when the children reached the clearing, they stopped short. Looking at each other, they both smiled. "Stories," Beno whispered. Allita nodded. "More stories," she said. The two of them sat down on the large, flat stone. And waited.

"Do you think the snake eats apples?" they asked each other.

Sure enough, the snake glided up and looked into their basket. "Greetings-s-s, my friends. Those apples-s-s look s-s-sweet!" it hissed.

"They are," Beno and Allita chorused.

"If you give me your apples-s-s, I'll tell you more s-s-stories," the snake said.

This time the children didn't hesitate. More than anything, they wanted to hear stories. "Oh yes, please," they replied.

And so once again the snake began to weave its tales. It told stories about how the first snake got its hiss and why the tortoise and hare aren't friends. Stories about how the world began and where the rainbow ends.

Finally, many tales later, the snake said, "I'm s-s-so hungry." Stretching its jaws wide, very wide, it began to swallow the apples one by one – gallumph, gallumph, gallumph. After many apples had disappeared, the snake stopped. Stuffed with apples from mouth to tail, the lumpy snake bumped slowly through the grass – ballumph, ballumph, ballumph – almost too heavy to move.

Beno and Allita picked up the half-empty basket and ran for home. It was late and their mother would be worried.

When Mama saw the apples in the bottom of the basket, she said, "Good. You've picked enough apples for a pie. Now don't tell me — the snake ate the rest of them."

The children put their hands over their mouths and giggled. But they said nothing about stories. Surely Mama wouldn't believe them.

That night the whole family ate hot apple pie for dessert. As Papa started on his second piece, he said, "What a strange sight I saw today on my way home! At the edge of the forest, I nearly stepped on a snake — the fattest, lumpiest snake imaginable. It was so fat it could hardly move!"

Beno and Allita began to laugh. In fact, they laughed so hard, they could barely gasp out, "Stories! Many, many stories!"

"Stories?" Mama and Papa were puzzled. "What are stories?"

With their eyes shining in the candlelight, the two children took turns retelling the snake's tales.

The very next day, Papa began to tell stories. He retold the snake's tales and then began to tell some of his own. First he told them to his goats. Then he told them to other goatherds, and those goatherds told stories to all their families and friends.

Mama began to weave stories into the tapestries she created. She told the stories to all who came to buy her weaving, and they told stories to their families and friends.

Through the years, Allita and Beno told stories, too, to anyone who would listen. And they always started each one with "This is a snake's tale."

SEASON AFTER SEASON, YEAR AFTER YEAR,
THE EARTH STILL TURNS FROM DAY TO NIGHT TO DAY. PEOPLE
STILL WORK AND EAT, SLEEP AND WAKE. BUT NOW THEY TELL
ONE ANOTHER STORIES, STORIES THAT CIRCLE THE EARTH AND
ARE PASSED DOWN FROM GENERATION TO GENERATION.

IF YOU EVER GO INTO A FOREST AND FIND A LARGE, FLAT
STONE JUST RIGHT TO REST UPON, SIT DOWN. WAIT. A SNAKE
JUST MIGHT APPEAR WITH NEW STORIES TO TELL. BUT BE SURE
TO BRING ALONG SOME FRESH FRUIT — PERHAPS STRAWBERRIES
OR RASPBERRIES. BUT NO APPLES.